World of Reading

LEVEL 3

SPIDEY'S NEW COSTUME

By Thomas Macri

Illustrated by Ramon Bachs *and* Hi-Fi Design

Based on the Marvel comic book series Spider-Man

New York
Los Angeles

marvelkids.com

© 2014 MARVEL

SUSTAINABLE FORESTRY INITIATIVE

Certified Chain of Custody
Promoting Sustainable Forestry

www.sfiprogram.org
SFI-01415

The SFI label applies to the text stock

Printed in the United States of America
First Edition
1 3 5 7 9 10 8 6 4 2
G658-7729-4-14046
ISBN 978-1-4231-5410-5

Chapter One:
Spidey's First Costume

Peter Parker was an ordinary kid who loved science. But his life was suddenly changed one day when he attended a demonstration. The experiment the scientists were doing involved radiation.

Just as the radioactive beams fired, a spider was zapped with the power. The spider fell, dying. It bit Peter before it died.

Before long he realized that the spider had given him fantastic powers. He could jump high. He could climb walls. And he even felt a tingling whenever he was in trouble. He called this his spider-sense, and it often saved him from danger.

Peter felt a great responsibility to use his powers to fight crime. But he couldn't go out in his street clothes, or people would recognize him. This could put his friends and family in danger. So he decided to create a costume.

He thought about what made him special. His spider powers, of course! He decided that the costume should remind people of a spider. But he didn't want to scare people.

He decided to make the costume bright red and blue. And he'd put spiderwebs on it and wear an image of a spider on his chest. He needed to cover his face, too. He created a tight mask. Even the eyes looked like markings on a spider.

There was still one thing a spider had that he didn't. Webs! Peter was a science expert, so he made a special fluid. Then he created devices to shoot the fluid. He called these his web-shooters. And when he shot fluid from them, he could spin webs.

Finally, his costume was done. Now all he needed was a name. And what better name was there for a man who had the powers of a spider than Spider-Man?

Chapter Two: Secret War

As Spider-Man, Peter fought villains. He kept New York City safe from crime. He protected as many people as he could. But he had help from other heroes. Teams like the Avengers, the X-Men, and the Fantastic Four helped Peter fight crime.

Once, all these Super Heroes found themselves instantly transported to a different world.

"This isn't Brooklyn, is it?" Spider-Man asked jokingly.

Soon the heroes discovered that they weren't the only ones who had been brought to that world. "We're under attack!" Spider-Man yelled.

Facing the heroes was a group of Earth's most dangerous villains. The being who had brought both groups to Battleworld to fight was called the Beyonder. It told the teams, "Defeat your enemies and all you desire shall be yours!"

The war was on! It was a secret war that no one on Earth was aware was happening. But it was still one of the greatest wars of all time.

It raged on, and both Super Heroes
and villains found their costumes
tattered and torn. What was worse was
that Spider-Man had run out of web
fluid. And he didn't have the chemicals
he needed to make more there on
Battleworld. Then Spider-Man noticed
Thor coming toward him.

"Hey, Thor! You got your cape back! And your hat! But how?" Spider-Man asked.

"T'was Hulk's doing. He used a device he discovered," Thor answered.

"Hulk think into it. It give Hulk new clothes!" the Hulk said. He sent Spider-Man into the fortress, where the device was.

Spider-Man noticed a bunch of machines inside.

"Which one is it?" he asked.

Then he noticed a black orb the size of a baseball floating in one device. He took it in his hand.

"Hey!" he shouted as a black material coming from the orb clung to his skin and moved up his arm.

Soon his entire body was covered with a new costume. And it was very different from his old one!

Chapter Three: Spidey's New Costume

"Check this out!" Spider-Man shouted.
"I've got my webs back!"

He jokingly fired a blast of web into
the face of his friend Johnny Storm
from the Fantastic Four.

"Where did you get these webs from?
They're even stronger than your old
ones!" Johnny said as he struggled to
rip the webs off his face.

"They're somehow built into
this new costume!" Spider-Man said.
"And that's not all—this suit does
anything! Watch this!" With a simple
thought, Spider-Man shortened his
sleeves and pantlegs.

"Short sleeves for summer!" he said.

Reed Richards, the brilliant scientist and leader of the Fantastic Four, said he'd love to examine the suit in his lab. That is, if they ever got back to Earth. And right then, he was working on a device that would do just that.

Just then, the ground was rocked. The heroes were under attack. Spider-Man had a chance to put his new costume to the test. He spun faster than

ever before. When his suit was torn, it repaired itself. And he never ran out of webbing. The suit made it easier for Spider-Man to fight. And it helped the heroes win the secret war!

When the battle was over, the heroes used the machine Hulk had found to fix their ruined costumes. But Spidey noticed that they weren't using the same machine he had to make his.

"Hey, guys! Do your suits do tricks? I mean, like, you know, respond to your thoughts and stuff?" he asked the other heroes.

"No, they're just...clothes," Johnny Storm said.

Oh well, Spider-Man thought. I must have just gotten lucky with mine!

Reed Richards's device was finally complete. He rounded up the heroes and sent them home a group at a time. All they had to do was think about where they wanted to go. Reed pointed the device at Peter. He pressed a button, and Spider-Man was on his way back to New York City!

Chapter Four: Back Home!

A blast of light filled the sky. From it, Spider-Man emerged. He was right in the middle of Central Park!

"Hey! You! What's going on?" a cop shouted at Spidey. "And who are you, anyway?"

"Me? I'm Spider-Man!" Peter answered.

"We've all seen Spider-Man before. You don't look a thing like him!" the cop answered.

Peter remembered then that he had his new costume on. No one on Earth had seen it yet. Another flash lit the sky just as the cops moved in on him. It was the Avengers. They'd made it back from Battleworld, too! Spidey slipped away while the cops watched the Avengers.

He swung over the city to his home in Queens. He dropped through the skylight. The first thing he wanted to do was change his clothes. But as he reached for his drawer, the costume transformed itself into a black shirt and jeans.

"The costume is responding to my thoughts again!" Peter said, smiling.

When he was ready for bed, the costume seemed to crawl off his body. It settled on a chair at the far side of his room. And when Peter woke in the middle of the night, the costume knew he wanted to do a little web-swinging. It covered him again.

"This new costume may be quick," he said. "But it'll be a long time before I get used to this!"

Peter did get used to his costume, though. He became comfortable in it. And it became easier to use.

But one night when he got home from web-slinging, the costume gave him trouble when he tried to take it off. The next night, it was even harder. And by the third night it took Peter almost an hour to get the costume off.

"Something's up," Peter said. "And I know just the doctor to give me a checkup."

Peter took the subway to Manhattan. Then he ducked into an alley. With a simple thought, the clothes he was wearing turned into his slick black suit.

I hope there's nothing wrong with the costume, Peter thought. It's so much easier to change into than the old one!

Chapter Five: Alive!

"Ah, Four Freedoms Plaza!" he said. "Home of the Fantastic Four! Reed Richards asked if he could check out my costume when we were back on Battleworld. With my costume acting so weird, this seems like a good time."

Spider-Man climbed up the side of the building and knocked on the window. Inside, Reed and Johnny Storm jumped a little. They were pretty high up for any visitors.

"Spider-Man!" Reed said. He motioned to the roof deck and let Spidey in.

"Is everything all right?" Reed asked.

"Not sure," Spider-Man said. "My new costume's been acting really weird."

Reed took him to his lab.

"I was hoping you'd take me up on my offer to examine it sooner," Reed said.

Reed ran test after test on the costume. With each test, he looked more concerned.

"Reed, what's wrong?" Spider-Man asked.

"It's almost too strange to believe," Reed said. "We all thought the costume was made of alien material. But it seems that it's much more than that. It appears the costume is an alien symbiote that has attached itself to you."

"You mean it's alive?" Spider-Man
shouted. "Get it off of me!" He started
leaping around the room, pulling at the
suit. "Yikes! I can't get it off! It's getting
tighter! It's crushing me!" he shouted.

"Many symbiotes are affected by sound!" Reed shouted. "We can use a sonic blaster!"

But by the time Reed had used his stretching power to grab the blaster, Spider-Man had swung off in a panic.

Johnny and Reed were right behind him.

"Where's he going?" Johnny asked.

"I suspect somewhere with a good deal of noise," Reed said.

Sure enough, Spider-Man was swooping toward City Cathedral! He landed in the bell tower. It was midnight, and the bells started to toll.

The sound hurt Spider-Man. He thought his ears would bleed. But he knew sound hurt the symbiote, too. So he had to stay there.

"It's working," Spider-Man said.
He could feel the suit loosening its grip.
But it was still hanging on tightly.
Spider-Man knew he had to keep
willing the suit off him. And time
was running out. The bells had just
tolled ten.

"Just two more..." Spider-Man said, thinking of the bells' loud toll. As soon as the sound stopped, the suit would tighten its grip again.

Then, with the twelfth ring, Peter managed to force the suit off him with his mind!

Just then, Reed and Johnny caught
up with Spider-Man.

Reed blasted the symbiote with
a ray. Then he trapped the suit in a
container.

"This will hold it until we can study it
further," Reed said.

"Aw, why are you covering your face? You can't be that ugly," Johnny joked.

"Give me a break, Johnny. You may not have a secret identity, but I do!" Spidey said.

"Then it's a good thing I brought this," Johnny said, tossing a red-and-blue suit toward Spider-Man. "We figured you'd need it if we trapped this alien thing."

It was his old costume. And Peter had never been so happy to see it!

"Thanks, pal," Spidey said as he ran behind a bell and suited up.

"Where are you off to now?" Reed asked.